Heroes and Villains of the Accipiter War: Illustrated

By Patrick Seaman

ISBN 979-8-9878511-5-9

MilStar Books
MILSTARBOOKS.COM
1st Edition, August 2023

3

<u>Forward</u>:

Step into the captivating universe of the Accipiter War science fiction book series. Within the pages of this book, you'll find a treasure trove of character dossiers and concept art, providing a glimpse into the minds of co-authors Patrick and Blake Seaman. This compilation offers just a taste of the vast story bible and extensive research that form the foundation of our ongoing series.

While we're excited to share these captivating visuals and character descriptions with you, we've taken care not to reveal too much. Our aim is to provide a tantalizing glimpse into the lives of the characters we hold dear without giving away all the surprises that await you in our thrilling narrative.

These dossiers are a version of what we pinned to our writer's wall, reminding us daily of the complexities and passions that define the characters we have created – and who we care greatly about. We are thrilled to share this window into their worlds, as it is their journeys that drive the heart of our narrative.

As you immerse yourself in these images and backgrounds, we hope they will ignite your imagination and kindle your curiosity about the unfolding Accipiter War saga. Please join us and our cast of characters as we embark upon a story of survival, love, politics, morality, and what promises to be a generational war against an ancient and vast empire that spans the entire galaxy.

Your journey begins here, and we can't wait to join you in this epic tale.

<u>About the Series:</u>

The novel is set in a post-apocalyptic world where an alien race called the Accipiters has attacked and conquered Earth. In the midst of the attack, a current-day Texas military town was snatched up by a mysterious alien race and placed inside a hollow 4,000-mile-long cylindrical world ship, complete with

Heroes and Villains of the Accipiter War: Illustrated

**Inspiration For The
Science Fiction Book Series by
Patrick and Blake Seaman**

oceans, continents, and shocking secrets. Now they must fight for survival and search for answers. Who brought them here and why? And what lies beyond the upward-curving horizon of this artificial world?

Amid an exploration of what it means to be human, this space opera / military science fiction series plunges readers headfirst into a fight for the survival of the human race and a war against an uncountable enemy. Book # 1 sets the stage for the series of books that follow that see our survivors take their battle to the stars, facing an enemy whose empire spans the galaxy.

The Characters:

The selected characters and art herein are in alphabetical order. To help maintain a bit of mystery about the story itself, and limit spoilers, we don't indicate which book in which any particular character appears.

Your journey begins here, and we can't wait to join you in this epic tale.

Audiobooks:

We are thrilled to announce that the audiobook version of "Accipiter War #1," narrated by the talented Michael Kramer, will be available later this year, offering readers another way to experience our immersive storytelling.

Hector Alonzo
Fort Brazos
Chief Deputy Sheriff

- Tour: 15 Years
- Marriage Status: Married
- Family: Wife Antonia, Children: Girls: Rocia, Celia, Reyna, Elena, Boys: Manuel, Vicente
- US Marine Veteran
- Education: Baylor University
- US Marine Corps Military Policeman
- Medal of Valor, SWAT Award
- 123 letters of commendation
- Height: 5' 10"
- Hair: Dark Brown
- Eyes: Brown
- Weight: 189lbs
- Age: 45
- Species: Human
- Sex: Male

Harrold Anders

U.S. Air Force
Chief Master Sargeant

- Tour: 15 Years
- Marriage Status: Single, three ex-wives
- Family: Extended family in Fort Brazos
- Active Duty U.S. Air Force, E-9
- Education: USAF Senior Non-commissioned Officer Academy
- Legion of Merit, Meritorious Service Medal with seven oak leaf clusters, Air Force Commendation Medal with three oak leaf clusters
- Height: 5' 10"
- Hair: Dark Brown
- Eyes: Grey
- Weight: 205lbs
- Age: 49
- Species: Human
- Sex: Male

Dr. Amelia Araki, M.D.
New London

- Lieutenant, United States Navy
- Doctor: USS Virginia (SSN-774
- Marriage Status: Single
- Family: None in Fort Brazos
- Education: Univ. of Hawaii, BS Marine Biology, MD from USU of the Health Sciences. Flight Surgeon. Naval Undersea Medical Institute. Board Certified in family, undersea & hyperbaric medicine.
- She enjoys surfing, scuba diving & hiking
- Height: 5' 5"
- Hair: Black
- Eyes: Black
- Weight: 122 lbs
- Age: 32
- Species: Human
- Sex: Female

John Austin
Sheriff
Fort Brazos

- Sheriff: Elected
- Marriage Status: Single, Widower
- Family: 8-year-old daughter Matilda
- Active Duty U.S. Air Force, E-9
- Education: MBA, Wharton; BS Petroleum Engineering, Texas A&M
- Patents: 3
- Self Made Man. Wife died a year ago.
- Donated new elementary school in her memory
- Height: 6' 2"
- Hair: Brown
- Eyes: Blue
- Weight: 195lbs
- Age: 45
- Species: Human
- Sex: Male

Mattilda Austin

Fort Brazos

- Daughter: John & Carolyn (deceased) Austin
- Mom died a year ago
- Family: 8-year-old daughter Matilda
- Education: Caroline Austin Elementary
- Horse: Appaloosa mare, Freckles, 14.2 hands
- Height: 4' 2"
- Hair: Dark blonde
- Eyes: Blue
- Weight: 52lbs
- Age: 8
- Species: Human
- Sex: Female

Dr. Jacob Becker, Ph.D.

Bonham State University
Fort Brazos

- Geneticist: Specialty: Genmod crops
- Marriage Status: Single
- Family: None in Fort Brazos
- Tenured Professor: Bonham State Univ.
- Education: Ph.D., Texas A&M Univ.
- Frequent clashes with Dr. Eva Sanches
- Height: 6' 1"
- Hair: Brown
- Eyes: Brown
- Weight: 196lbs
- Age: 55
- Species: Human
- Sex: Male

Sybil Blanchard

Fort Brazos

- Truck Driver
- Marriage Status: Married
- Family: Husband: Wayne Blanchard
- Education: B.A., Business Administration, Oklahoma State Univ.
- Manages family trucking business
- Height: 5' 3"
- Hair: Long curly dark frizzy hair
- Eyes: Brown
- Weight: 101 lbs
- Age: 37
- Species: Human
- Sex: Female

Wayne Blanchard

Fort Brazos

- Truck Driver
- Marriage Status: Married
- Family: Wife, Truck Driver Sybil Blanchard
- Education: B.S. ME, Texas A&M Univ.
- Army Veteran: Managed logistics
- Has a half dozen other drivers and rigs
- Height: 5' 11"
- Hair: Brown
- Eyes: Brown
- Weight: 220 lbs
- Age: 39
- Species: Human
- Sex: Male

Colonel Gaspard Xavier Boyer

Fort Brazos

- French Expeditionary Infantry Officer
- Marriage Status: Single
- Family: Father and Grandfather both served in the French military
- Height: 5' 10"
- Hair: Dark Brown
- Eyes: Brown
- Weight: 172 lbs
- Age: 36
- Species: Human
- Sex: Male

Ray Bunker
Fort Brazos

- Assistant Mgr, Reinhardt Distributing
- Marriage Status: Married
- Family: Wife Julie, Daughter Chloe, Ray is foster brother to Gary Litte
- Played HS football w/Garry Little and Darnell Lewis
- Army Veteran
- Prepper
- Height: 6' 1"
- Hair: Black
- Eyes: Hazle
- Weight: 190 lbs
- Age: 29
- Species: Human
- Sex: Male

Sabrina Chiton
Brigadier General
Fort Brazos

- Brigadier General, British Army
- Royal Corps of Signals ("Royal Signals")
- Marriage Status: Widow
- Family: Daughter: Nicole, Age 14
- Height: 5' 8"
- Hair: Blonde (greying)
- Eyes: Soft Blue
- Weight: 115 lbs
- Age: 44
- Species: Human
- Sex: Female

Commander Choe Pyong-Chol

Fort Brazos

- North Korean Maritime Special Purpose Forces, 34th Army Navy Sniper Brigade
- Marriage Status: Single
- Father and grandfather served in the North Korean military
- Height: 5' 8"
- Hair: Black
- Eyes: Dark Brown
- Weight: 180 lbs
- Age: 35
- Species: Human
- Sex: Male

Esmerelda Collins

Fort Brazos

- City Councilwoman,
- Owner: Collins Ranch
- Marriage Status: Single. Divorced
- Godmother to Sandra Hoffman
- Education: MBA, Texas A&M University
- Family was among the original settlers
- Height: 5' 6"
- Hair: Brown, long
- Eyes: Hazle
- Weight: 138 lbs
- Age: 42
- Species: Human
- Sex: Female

Charles Cross

New London

- Commanding: SSN-785 John Warner
- Marriage Status: Single
- Family: Only child
- Education: OCS, Ph.D. in Physics and a Masters Degree in Electrical Engineering
- Family was among the original settlers
- Height: 5' 11"
- Hair: Brown
- Eyes: Grey
- Weight: 188 lbs
- Age: 42
- Species: Human
- Sex: Male

Jermaine Cutter

New London

- CO: SSN-795 Hyman G. Rickover
- Marriage Status: Single
- Family: Only child, Wealthy Family
- Education: Annapolis. MS in Electrical Engineering, Nuclear Power School (NPS)
- Plays piano and sails a Catalina 309
- Height: 6' 1"
- Hair: Black
- Eyes: Black
- Weight: 192 lbs
- Age: 39
- Species: Human
- Sex: Male

Roxanna Darling

Fort Brazos

- Corporal, United States Marines
- Marriage Status: Single
- Family: Only child, Iranian + Mexican
- Education: High School Graduate
- Plays piano and sails a Catalina 309
- Height: 5' 6"
- Hair: Black/Brown, Ponytail
- Eyes: Brown
- Weight: 127 lbs
- Age: 24
- Species: Human
- Sex: Female

Dr. David Duncan, M.D.

Fort Brazos

- Surgeon, Methodist Hospital
- Marriage Status: Single
- Family: None in Fort Brazos
- Former US Army doctor.
- Education: MD, John's Hopkins, West Point Graduate
- Often plays golf with Mayor Parker
- Height: 5' 11"
- Hair: Brown
- Eyes: Brown
- Weight: 192 lbs
- Age: 37
- Species: Human
- Sex: Male

Dr. Gwyneth Elliot M.D.

Fort Brazos

- Doctor, U.S. Navy, Surgeon
- Frederick Fuller Russell Medical Center
- Marriage Status: Single
- Family: None in Fort Brazos
- Education: M.D. Uniformed Services University F. Edward Hébert School of Medicine, Bethesda, Maryland
- Former Olympic Biathlon USA Silver medal winner
- Height: 5' 4"
- Hair: Red
- Eyes: Hazle
- Weight: 132 lbs
- Age: 39
- Species: Human
- Sex: Female

Capt. Gail Finley
Fort Brazos

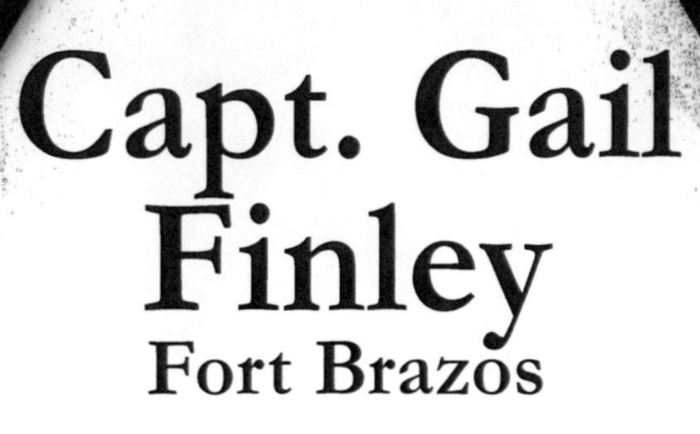

- Captain, U.S. Air Force
- Pilot: EA-18, F-15, F-35
- Marriage Status: Single
- Family: None in Fort Brazos
- Education: BS/MS in Aeronautical Eng., California Poly State University
- Flew 89 combat missions
- Height: 5' 9"
- Hair: Auburn
- Eyes: Green
- Weight: 126 lbs
- Age: 32
- Species: Human
- Sex: Female

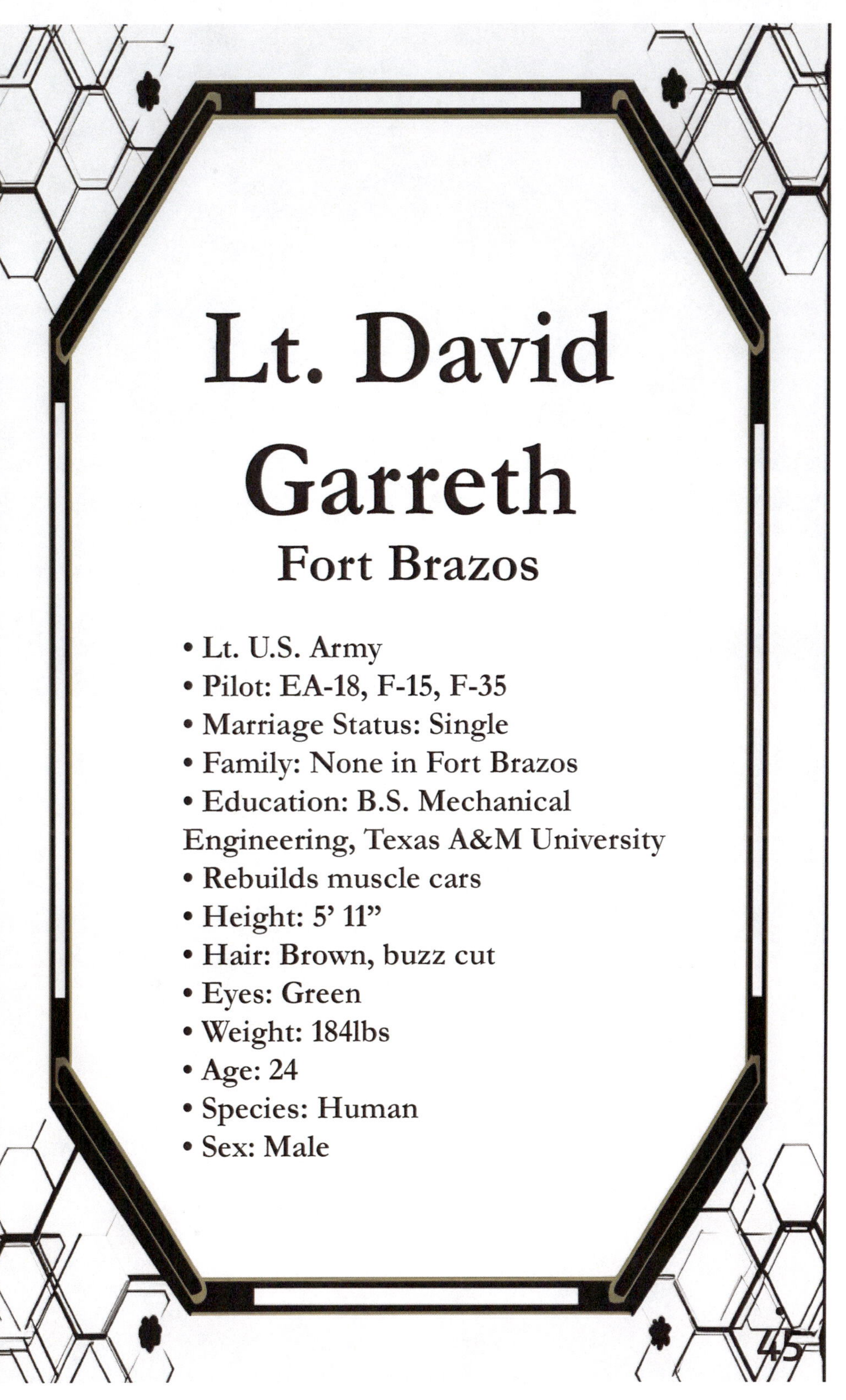

Lt. David Garreth

Fort Brazos

- Lt. U.S. Army
- Pilot: EA-18, F-15, F-35
- Marriage Status: Single
- Family: None in Fort Brazos
- Education: B.S. Mechanical Engineering, Texas A&M University
- Rebuilds muscle cars
- Height: 5' 11"
- Hair: Brown, buzz cut
- Eyes: Green
- Weight: 184lbs
- Age: 24
- Species: Human
- Sex: Male

Joseph Gilmore

Fort Brazos

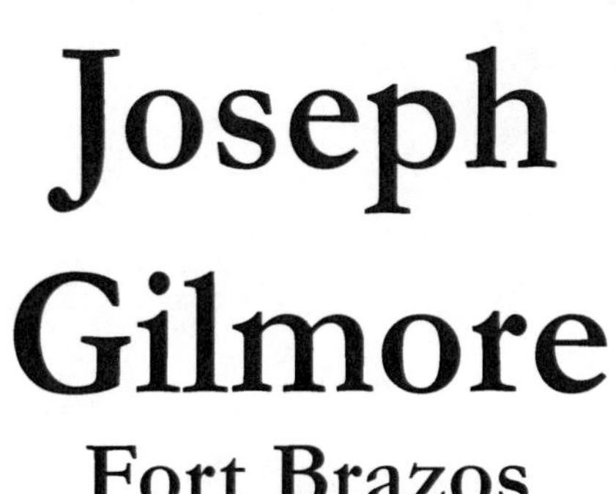

- Pastor, First United Methodist Church
- Marriage Status: Widower
- Family: None in Fort Brazos
- Education: Doctor of Divinity, Vanderbilt University
- Author of 28 books
- Height: 6' 2"
- Hair: White
- Eyes: Blue
- Weight: 183lbs
- Age: 68
- Species: Human
- Sex: Male

Lt. Alister Gordon

New London

- Lt. U.S. Navy
- Marriage Status: Single
- Family: None in Fort Brazos
- Education: Officer Training Command (OTC)
- He has a tattoo of a Celtic knot on his left arm and a scar on his right cheek from a knife fight
- Height: 5' 8"
- Hair: Blonde
- Eyes: Blue
- Weight: 148lbs
- Age: 32
- Species: Human
- Sex: Male

Capt. Valentin Gorshkov
Fort Brazos

- Russian Federation Naval Infantry
- Marriage Status: Single
- Family: None in Fort Brazos
- Expert in marine engineering and is skilled in operating a wide range of military hardware, including tanks, artillery, and aircraft. Proficient in hand-to-hand combatant and an expert in small arms
- Height: 6' 0"
- Hair: Short Black
- Eyes: Blue
- Weight: 192lbs
- Age: 32
- Species: Human
- Sex: Male

Nathaniel Grant

Fort Brazos

- Former US Navy Nuclear Engineer
- Marriage Status: Married
- Family: Family: Wife Jasmine & Daughters Aiysha and Malaika
- Education: Naval Postgraduate School, M.S. Mechanical Engineering, Bettis Reactor Engineering School, Thomas Edison State University
- Height: 6' 0"
- Hair: Black
- Eyes: Black
- Weight: 185 lbs
- Species: Human
- Sex: Male

Lt. Darryl Guevara

Fort Brazos

- United States Air Force
- Marriage Status: Widower
- Family: Wife Amara, 2 year old girl Aneesha, 1 year old girl Aletha
- Education: Masters Degree, Avionics, Florida State University
- Pastimes: Motorcycle riding, Plays electric guitar, Baseball
- Height: 5' 11"
- Hair: Black
- Eyes: Brown
- Weight: 175 lbs
- Species: Human
- Sex: Male

Cdr. Thomas Harding

New London

- United States Navy
- Operations Research Analyst, Office of the Secretary of Defense
- Deputy, Nuclear Propulsion Program Mgr
- Marriage Status: Single
- Family: None in Fort Brazos
- Education: M.B.A., U. of Florida, B.S. Math and Computer Science, U. of Idaho
- Writing a book on the British and French wars between 1793 and 1815.
- Height: 5' 10"
- Hair: Grey
- Eyes: Grey
- Weight: 205 lbs
- Species: Human
- Sex: Male

Francis (Frank) Hayes

Fort Brazos

- Texas Rangers: Retired
- Marriage Status: Widower
- Family: None in Fort Brazos
- Education: Baylor University
- Actively consults with local and national law enforcement on special cases
- Height: 5' 9"
- Hair: Grey
- Eyes: Hazle
- Weight: 168 lbs
- Species: Human
- Sex: Male

Lt. Cdr Ramona Henry

New London

- Marriage Status: Single
- Family: None in Fort Brazos
- Education: BS ME, M.I.T., MS Nuclear Engineering, University of Cambridge, MS Naval Architecture, US Naval Academy
- Nuclear Power School Graduate
- Advanced Submarine Warfare Officer Course, United States Navy, Graduated from the U.S. Naval Academy. Master's Thesis on Thorium Fueled Nuclear Reactor Concepts
- Age: 34
- Height: 5' 9"
- Hair: Strawberry Blonde
- Eyes: Watery Blue
- Weight: 141 lbs
- Species: Human
- Sex: Female

Sandra Hoffman
Fort Brazos

- Councilman Barrett Hoffman's daughter
- Marriage Status: Single
- Family: Large family in Fort Brazos
- Education: Attending Fort Brazos HS
- The Hoffman family ranch is a 100 year old ranch and dairy farm. The Hoffman's are part one of the founding families of Fort Brazos
- Sandra has won many trophies in Track
- Age: 17
- Height: 5' 10"
- Hair: Long Blonde
- Eyes: Blue
- Weight: 114 lbs
- Species: Human
- Sex: Female

Dale Hubbard

Fort Brazos

- City Councilman
- Car Dealership Owner
- Marriage Status: Married
- Family: Extended family in Fort Brazos
- Education: BA Business Administration, Bonham State Univerity
- After college, Dale opened a car dealership with his brother. Over the years, the dealership grew and became one of the most successful in the area. He has been on the City Council for 12 years.
- Age: 60
- Height: 5' 10"
- Hair: Long Blonde
- Eyes: Blue
- Weight: 178 lbs
- Species: Human
- Sex: Male

Ignacio
Fort Brazos

- Columbian Mercenary
- Marriage Status: Single
- Family: None in Fort Brazos
- Leader of a band of 175 mercenaries of mostly south American origin. The group is known as 'Ignacio' or sometimes 'Ignacio's Legion'
- Age: 32
- Height: 5' 10"
- Hair: Brown
- Eyes: Brown
- Weight: 158 lbs
- Species: Human
- Sex: Male

Colonel P'aeng Jin-Hwan

Fort Brazos

- Colonel (Daechwa) P'aeng Jin-Hwan
- North Korean Maritime Special Purpose Forces, 34th Army Navy Sniper Brigade
- Marriage Status: Single
- His father, a revered General, was executed for giving extra rations to his men. As a result, Jin-Hwan mercilessly drills his men.
- Height: 5' 8"
- Hair: Black
- Eyes: Dark Brown
- Weight: 180 lbs
- Age: 35
- Species: Human
- Sex: Male

Rear Adm. Andre Johansson
New London

- Rear Admiral Lower Half, US Navy
- Family: Son: Karl, Wife: Sofie
- Education: Summa Cum Laude from UCLA Physics, History and PoliSci, Naval Academy Graduate, Graduate of Nuclear Power School
- Captained USS Asheville SSN-758 as a division officer, USS Miami SSN-755 as the Combat Systems Officer, and USS GEORGIA (SSGN 729) as Executive Officer
- Age: 51
- Height: 5' 11"
- Weight: 191 lbs
- Hair: Grey
- Eyes: Grey
- Species: Human
- Sex: Male

Karl

Johansson
New London
- Marriage Status: Single
- Family: Father: Andre, Mother: Sofie
- Education: All-State linebacker, University of Connecticut
- Age: 20
- Height: 6' 2"
- Weight: 210 lbs
- Hair: Grey
- Eyes: Grey
- Species: Human
- Sex: Male

The Keeper

Darnell Lewis

Fort Brazos

- Assistant Manager, Reinhardt Distributing
- Marriage Status: Single
- Family: Mom Jasmine and sister Yazmeen
- Played HS football on same team as Garry Little and Ray Bunker. Promising college Running Back, cut short in freshman year after a severe fracture.
- Height: 5' 10"
- Hair: Black
- Eyes: Brown
- Weight: 212 lbs
- Age: 28
- Species: Human
- Sex: Male

Gary Little
Fort Brazos

- Driver, Reinhardt Distributing
- Marriage Status: Married
- Family: Wife Darlene
- Played HS football on same team as Garry Little and Darnell Lewis.
- Was a womanizer before Darlene
- Prepper. Has specialty knowledge and gear
- Height: 6' 0"
- Hair: Brown
- Eyes: Blue
- Weight: 192 lbs
- Age: 27
- Species: Human
- Sex: Male

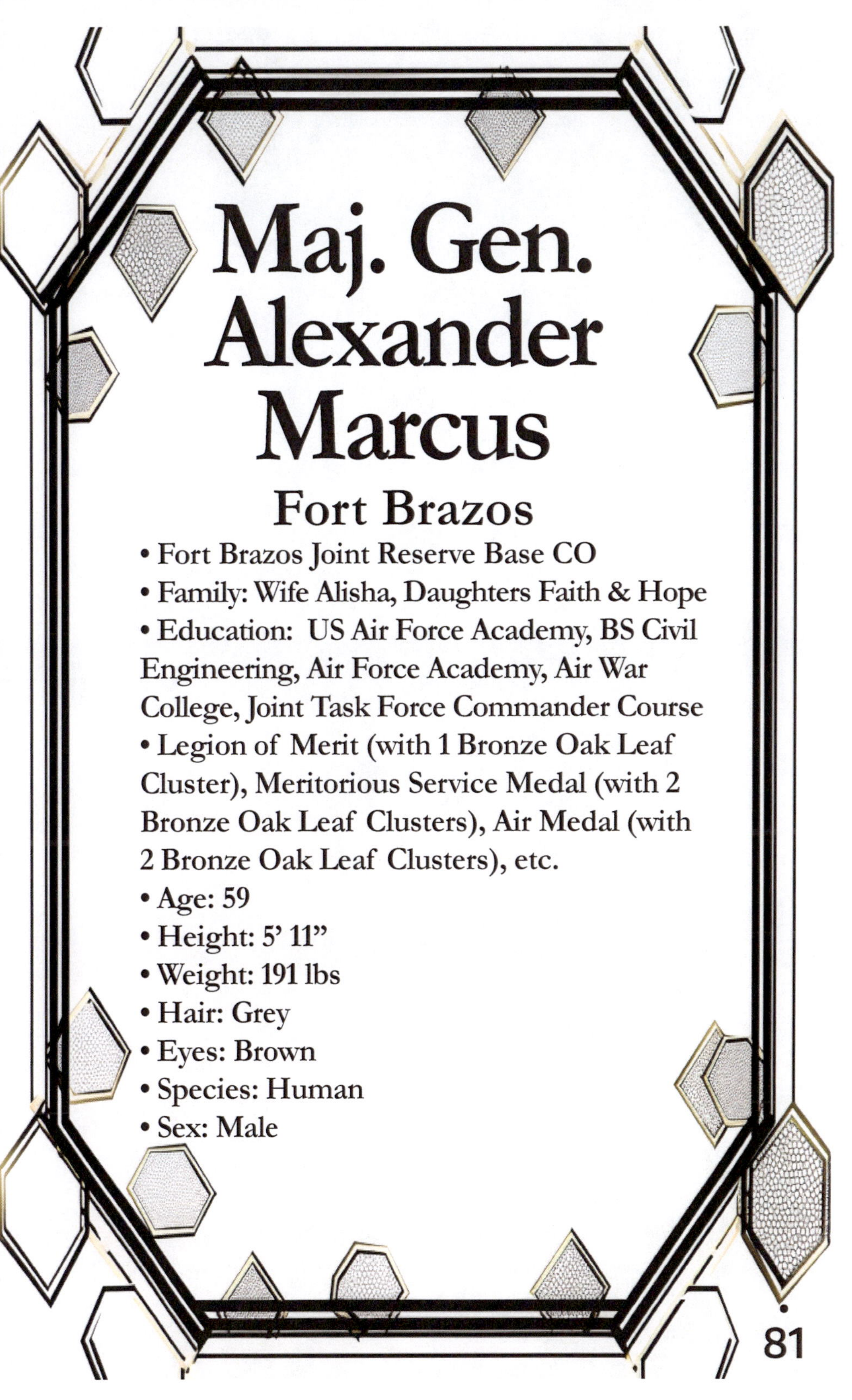

Maj. Gen. Alexander Marcus

Fort Brazos

- Fort Brazos Joint Reserve Base CO
- Family: Wife Alisha, Daughters Faith & Hope
- Education: US Air Force Academy, BS Civil Engineering, Air Force Academy, Air War College, Joint Task Force Commander Course
- Legion of Merit (with 1 Bronze Oak Leaf Cluster), Meritorious Service Medal (with 2 Bronze Oak Leaf Clusters), Air Medal (with 2 Bronze Oak Leaf Clusters), etc.
- Age: 59
- Height: 5' 11"
- Weight: 191 lbs
- Hair: Grey
- Eyes: Brown
- Species: Human
- Sex: Male

Lt. Gen. Gideon Marcovic

Fort Brazos

- Colonel, IDF 188th Barak Armored Brigade
- Family: Wife Carmit, daughters Anat & Brach
- Education: Bar-Ilan Univ: BA Comm. & PoliSci, Summa Cum Laude; Barak Aroc Command & General Staff Academy, High Rank Officers Program
- Avid football (soccer) player & cook
- Age: 38
- Height: 5' 10"
- Weight: 156 lbs
- Hair: Brown
- Eyes: Brown
- Species: Human
- Sex: Male

Livia Milner
New London

- Full partner at Connally, Gibson and Sullivan, in Washington D.C.
- Family: Husband VADM Preston Milner, Twin sister, Isadora, Daughter: Helena, Father: Senior Senator from Massachusetts, mother is a judge on the 1st Circuit Court of Appeals in Boston.
- Education: LL.M. The Master of Laws (LL.M.), Yale
- Age: 39
- Height: 5' 6"
- Weight: 119 lbs
- Hair: Long, Black
- Eyes: Jade Green
- Species: Human
- Sex: Female

Vice Admiral Preston Stewart Milner, III
New London

- US Deputy Chief of Naval Operations
- Married: Livia Milner, daughter: Helena
- Education: U.S. Naval Academy: BS EE, MS EE, Weapons Systems Engineering from the Naval Postgraduate School.
- Served aboard both attack and ballistic missile submarines. Commanded USS Maryland (SSBN 738) and was Commodore of Submarine Development Squadron 10
- Pastimes: Rowing, Sailing, Golf, Tennis
- Age: 51
- Height: 5' 11"
- Weight: 198 lbs
- Hair: Grey
- Eyes: Grey
- Species: Human

Mara Morhouse

Fort Brazos

- Senior IT Network Engineer
- Marriage Status: Single
- Education: BS Computer Science, Networking & Systems, UT Austin
- Volunteers with STEM education and mentorship programs for underrepresented youth. Also, an avid reader, with a love for science fiction and fantasy novels, is an avid D&D player and is fascinated by mythology.
- Age: 28
- Height: 5' 6"
- Weight: 140 lbs
- Hair: Dark brown
- Eyes: Brown
- Species: Human
- Sex: Female

CDR Eugene Morton
New London

- Commander SSN-795 Hyman G. Rickover
- Marriage Status: Single
- Education: U.S. Naval Academy: BS EE, MS EE, Weapons Systems Engineering from the Naval Postgraduate School, Nuclear Power School (NPS)
- Pastimes: Chess, astronomy, classic and naval literature and history, scuba diving,
- Age: 37
- Height: 5' 11"
- Weight: 198 lbs
- Hair: Grey
- Eyes: Grey
- Species: Human
- Sex: Male

Dr. Takumi Nakamura, Ph.D.

Fort Brazos

- Dean, School of Science and Technology, Bonham State University. Tenured.
- Marriage Status: Married
- Family: Wife Mizuki, Children Naomi, Misaki, Katsumi, and Fumio
- Education: Ph.D., University of Texas
- Has discovered three comets in his spare time, published many peer-reviewed papers and research. Grows Japanese vegetables in an aquaponic vertical garden
- Age: 54
- Height: 5' 6"
- Weight: 135 lbs
- Hair: Grey with streaks of black
- Eyes: Grey
- Species: Human
- Sex: Male

Dr. Patrick O'Connell, Ph.D.

Fort Brazos

- Dean, School of Science and Technology, Bonham State University. Tenured
- Marriage Status: Widower
- Family: None in Fort Brazos
- Education: Ph.D. in Quantum Physics and Nanotechnology, Texas A&M University
- Pastimes: Hiking, Astonomy & Molecular Gastronomy
- Age: 63
- Height: 5' 10"
- Weight: 175 lbs
- Hair: Grey
- Eyes: Grey
- Species: Human
- Sex: Male

Dr. Hyun Park, Ph.D.

Fort Brazos

- VP Logistics, Korea Shipbuilding & Offshore Engineering Co., Ltd. and Professor at Seoul National University.
- Marriage Status: Married
- Family: Wife Areum and daughters Gi, Iseul, Myeong, Nari and Uk.
- Education: BS, MS & Ph.D. in Industrial Engineering: KAIST Korea Advanced Institute of Science and Technology
- Pastimes: Photography, Gardening, Reading, Mentoring, Travel, Playing Piano, gayageum and janggu, and, privately, Taekwondo
- Age: 56
- Height: 5' 10" (178 cm)
- Weight: 175 lbs (79 kg)
- Hair Color: Salt-and-pepper black
- Eye Color: Warm brown

Lt. CDR Lorraine Parker

New London

- EDO, SSN-795 Hyman G. Rickover
- Marriage Status: Single
- Family: None
- Education: Ph.D. EE from MIT, Naval Construction and Engineering
Nuclear Engineering, US Naval Academy, Nuclear Power School (NPS)
- Pastimes: Running and weightlifting. She also enjoys reading science fiction and is a big fan of Star Trek.
- Age: 36
- Height: 5' 8"
- Weight: 132 lbs
- Hair Color: Black
- Eye Color: Purple
- Species: Human
- Sex: Female

Mayor Tom Parker

Fort Brazos

- Mayor (4th Term), car dealership owner
- Marriage Status: Married
- Family: wife, grown children in Fort Brazos
- Education: MBA, Texas Christian University
- Led effort to move military units to the Fort Brazos military base, avoiding a shutdown
- 2nd generation owner of one of the oldest Ford car dealerships in Texas
- Senior Deacon at Church
- Was High School football star quarterback Wife is a former Kilgore Rangerette and Miss Texas runner up
- Age: 56
- Height: 5' 11"
- Weight: 178 lbs
- Hair Color: Grey
- Eye Color: Green
- Species: Human
- Sex: Male

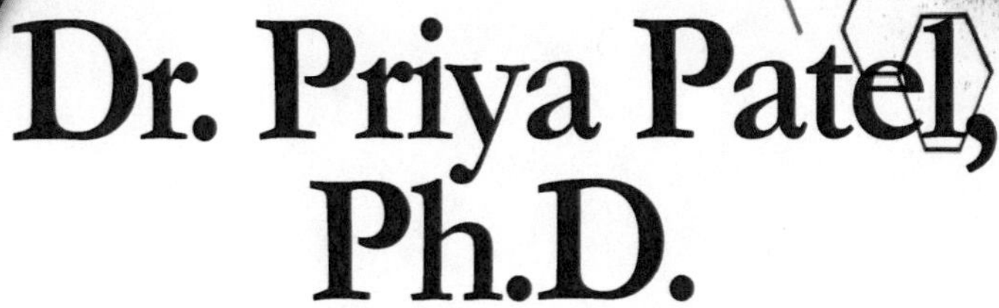

Dr. Priya Patel, Ph.D.

Fort Brazos

- Dean, Physics Department, Bonham State University. Tenured. Previously Assitant Professor of Physics, US Military Academy
- Marriage Status: Married
- Family: Husband: Aryan (Lawyer), Children: Son: Arjun, Daughter: Maya.
- Education: Ph.D. Physics, U of North Texas, MS Physics, BS EE, U of Houston
- Published 50+ papers in prestigious journals & received several grants and honors
- Age: 42
- Height: 5' 3"
- Weight: 111 lbs
- Hair: Dark brown hair
- Eyes: Brown
- Species: Human
- Sex: Female

Danielle Richardson
Fort Brazos

- Radio Host / Disk Jockey, 92.5 FM
- Marriage Status: Single
- Family: None in Fort Brazos
- Education: BA Journalism, U of Oklahoma
- Most recognized radio voice in Fort Brazos
- Billboards with her face advertise the station
- Free-form radio – whatever she feels like doing
- Age: 36
- Height: 5' 6"
- Weight: 112 lbs
- Hair: Black with accents
- Eyes: Grey
- Species: Human
- Sex: Female

Lt. Ryon Ki-Nam

Fort Brazos

- North Korean Maritime Special Purpose Forces, 34th Army Navy Sniper Brigade
- Marriage Status: Single
- As a sniper within the North Korean Maritime Special Purpose Forces, Lieutenant Ryon Ki-Nam specializes in maritime operations, executing precision long-range shots from concealed positions. He is highly trained in coastal defense, intelligence gathering, and supporting special operations in challenging maritime environments
- Birthplace: Pyongyang, North Korea
- Height: 5 feet 10 inches (178 cm)
- Weight: 170 lbs (77 kg)
- Eye Color: Dark Brown
- Hair Color: Black
- Species: Human
- Sex: Male

Col. Caesar Salangsang

Fort Brazos

- Colonel, Philippine Army 54th Engineering Brigade
- Marriage Status: Single
- Family: Wife Maria, Children Gabriel, Isabella, Lucas, Mateo, Sofia, Elena, Rafael, Alejandro, and Camila
- Pastimes: Milsim Games, Family time, Military History, Travel, Golf, Sailing
- Education: Philippine Military Academy
- Height: 5 feet 10 inches (178 cm)
- Weight: 170 lbs (77 kg)
- Eye Color: Dark Brown
- Hair Color: Black
- Species: Human
- Sex: Male

Eva Sanches DVM

Fort Brazos

- Owner: Sanches Veterinary & Equine Center
- Specialty: Large Animals
- Marriage Status: Single
- Family: Extended family in Fort Brazos
- Took over father's Veterinary Clinic
- Strong reputation as miracle worker
- Political Activist for social causes
- Works closely with Ag programs at Bonham State University
- Frequently clashes with Dr. Jacob Becker
- Education: D.V.M. Texas A&M University
- Age: 45
- Height: 5 feet 2 inches
- Weight: 102 lbs
- Eye Color: Black
- Hair Color: Black
- Species: Human
- Sex: Female

CDR Alberta Sinitskaya
New London

- Supervisor of Shipbuilding, Conversion and Repair, Groton
- Marriage Status: Married
- Family: Husband Dimitri, Children: Ronald (17) and Anna (19)
- Education: Oceanography US Naval Academy, Naval Postgraduate School. MS Engineering Acoustics. Warfare Officer Qualification aboard USS Delaware (SSN-791), followed USS Illinois (SSN-786)
- Rides & Repairs her Harley Davidson
- Age: 42
- Height: 5 feet 2 inches
- Weight: 102 lbs
- Eye Color: Black
- Hair Color: Black
- Species: Human
- Sex: Female

Dr. Dimitri Sinitskaya, Ph.D.

New London

- Principal Engineer, Bechtel Group
- Wife: Alberta, Children: Ronald and Anna
- Education: BS, MS, Ph.D. EE, MIT
- Published numerous papers in top-tier academic journals. Is a skilled programmer. • Pastimes: Hiking, riding motorcycles with wife Bertie. Courtesy of his grandfather, he is an avid chess player. He is fluent in both English and Russian and enjoys reading Russian literature.
- Age: 49
- Height: 6 feet 1 inches
- Weight: 193 lbs
- Eye Color: Green
- Hair Color: Dark Brown
- Species: Human
- Sex: Male

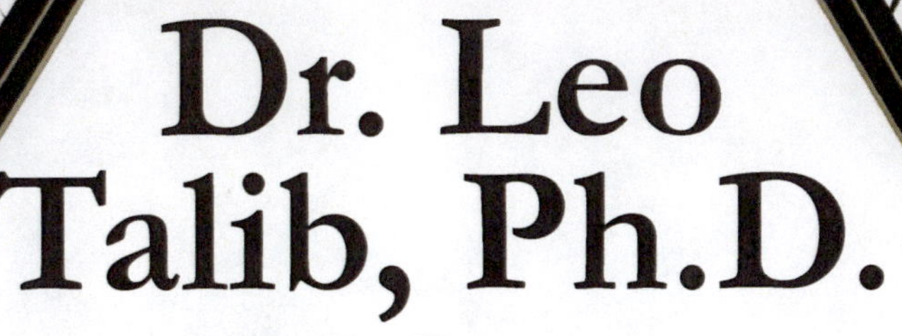

Dr. Leo Talib, Ph.D.

Fort Brazos

- Assistant Dean of Language Studies Bonham State University
- Marriage Status: Single
- Family: None in Fort Brazos
- Education: Ph.D. Boston University
- Diplomat parents. Never in one place long, he grew up in Algiers, Paris, Brussels, Bogota, Beijing, London, Washington D.C.
- Polyglot, fluent in twenty-six languages and passable in a dozen more
- Pastimes: Tennis, Rowing, Antiquities
- Clothing: Saville Rowe
- IQ: Approximately 200
- Age: 35
- Height: 5' 10"
- Weight: 172 lbs
- Eye Color: Brown
- Hair Color: Brown
- Species: Human
- Sex: Male

CDR Philip "Phil" Underwood

New London

- CO: SSN-797 Iowa, SSN-795 Hyman G. Rickover
- Marriage Status: Single
- Family: Only child, Wealthy Family
- Education: Annapolis. Masters Degree in Electrical Engineering, Nuclear Power School
- Former Quarterback for US Navy FB Team
- Fanatical about training and drilling to build team confidence and performance
- Height: 6' 0"
- Hair: Dark brown to black hair
- Eyes: Grey
- Weight: 183 lbs
- Age: 41
- Species: Human
- Sex: Male

Gloria Vargas
Fort Brazos

- City Councilwoman, Jewelry store owner and Southwest Art Museum owner
- Marriage Status:Divorced twice. Third husband died suddenly
- Family: No Children, but extended family in Fort Brazos. Hispanic and American Indian
- Education: BA, Austin College
- Paints southwestern-style landscapes
- Proponent on City Council for maintaining history and heritage over development.
- Height: 5' 2"
- Hair: Long black, mostly turned silver
- Eyes: brown
- Weight: 104 lbs
- Age: 52
- Species: Human
- Sex: Female

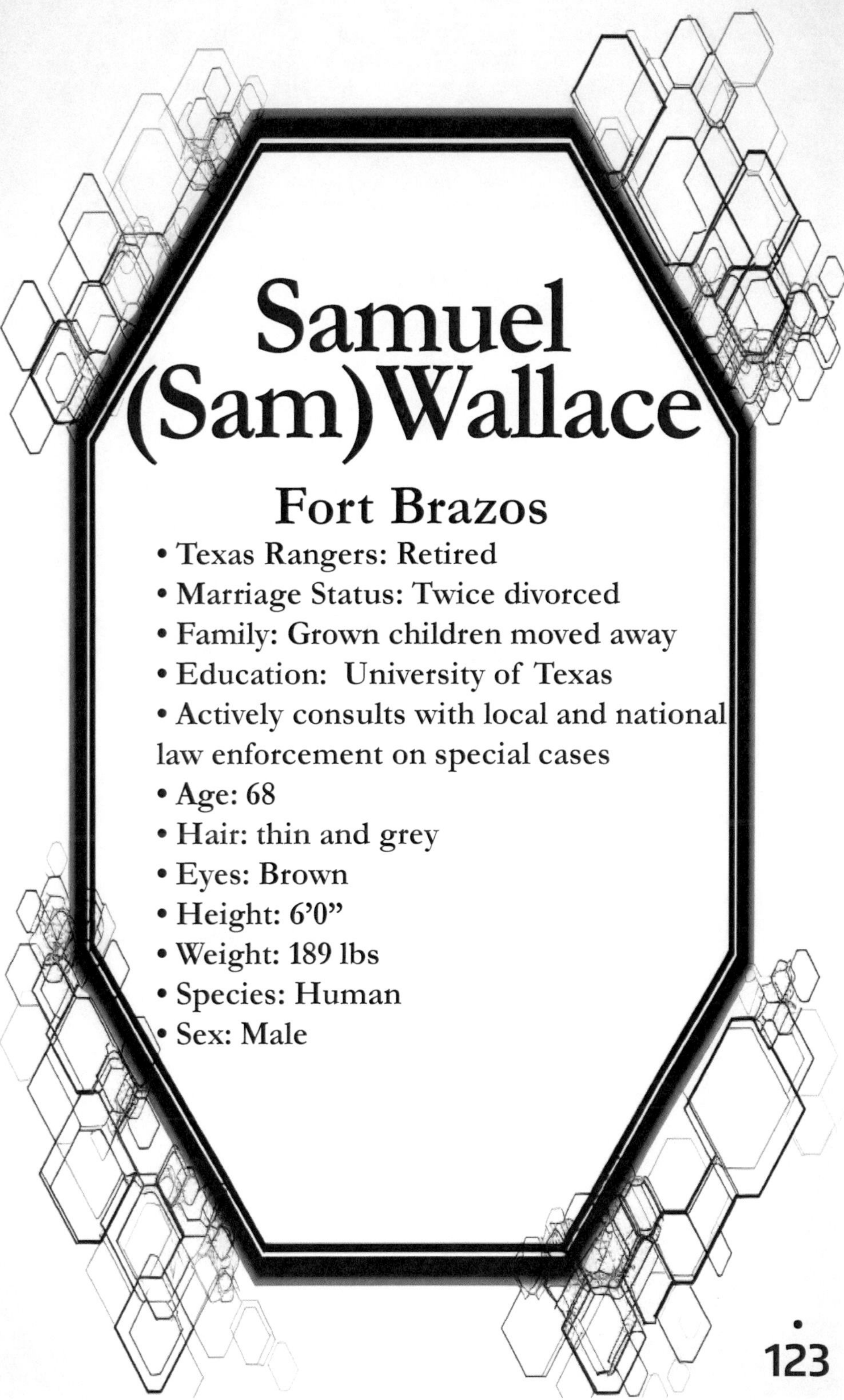

Samuel (Sam) Wallace

Fort Brazos

- Texas Rangers: Retired
- Marriage Status: Twice divorced
- Family: Grown children moved away
- Education: University of Texas
- Actively consults with local and national law enforcement on special cases
- Age: 68
- Hair: thin and grey
- Eyes: Brown
- Height: 6'0"
- Weight: 189 lbs
- Species: Human
- Sex: Male

Lt. Col. Martin Williams

Fort Brazos

- Australian Secret Intelligence Service
- Marriage Status: Single
- Family: None in Fort Brazos
- Education: Master of International Studies, University of Sydney
- Has worked in the Middle East and other, exotic, places. He strives to look like an overworked, uninspired accountant.
- Age: 41
- Hair: Varies, depending
- Eyes: Brown
- Height: 5' 8"
- Weight: 178 lbs
- Species: Human
- Sex: Male

Mira Yaeger
Fort Brazos

- Manages an insurance agency
- Marriage Status: Widow
- Family: Father, Frank
- Education: MBA: Texas Christian Univ.
- At 9, Mira lost her mother to cancer & was raised by her banker and big game hunter father, Frank. Mira is an accomplished big game hunter herself.
- Age: 32
- Hair: Wavy dirty blonde
- Eyes: Brown
- Height: 5' 10"
- Weight: 178 lbs
- Species: Human
- Sex: Female

CDR Rafferty Youngman
New London

- Commanding USS Illinois SSN-800
- Marriage Status: Married, Anna, with two children, Robert and Clara
- Family: Grew up in a military family, with his father serving in the Navy as well
- Education: Annapolis. MS EE, Nuclear Power School (NPS)
- Pastimes: sailing, woodworking, military history. Volunteers w/a youth sailing program
- Age: 38
- Hair: Brown
- Eyes: Brown
- Height: 5' 11"
- Weight: 192 lbs
- Species: Human
- Sex: Male

Mei Zifeng

Fort Brazos

- Botony Post Graduate Student, BSU
- Marriage Status: Single
- Family: Only child. Father: Ambassador Zifeng, serving in the Chinese Foreign Service. Mother: Dr. Lin, a renowned cultural anthropologist and consultant
- Education: BS Biology, Beijing University, China, MS Botany, BSU
- Growing up in a diplomatic household, Mei developed multilingual skills. She speaks Mandarin Chinese, English, French, and German fluently
- Age: 24
- Hair: Black
- Eyes: Brown
- Height: 5' 2"
- Weight: 105 lbs
- Species: Human
- Sex: Female

WARDOG

STALKER

ACCIPITER

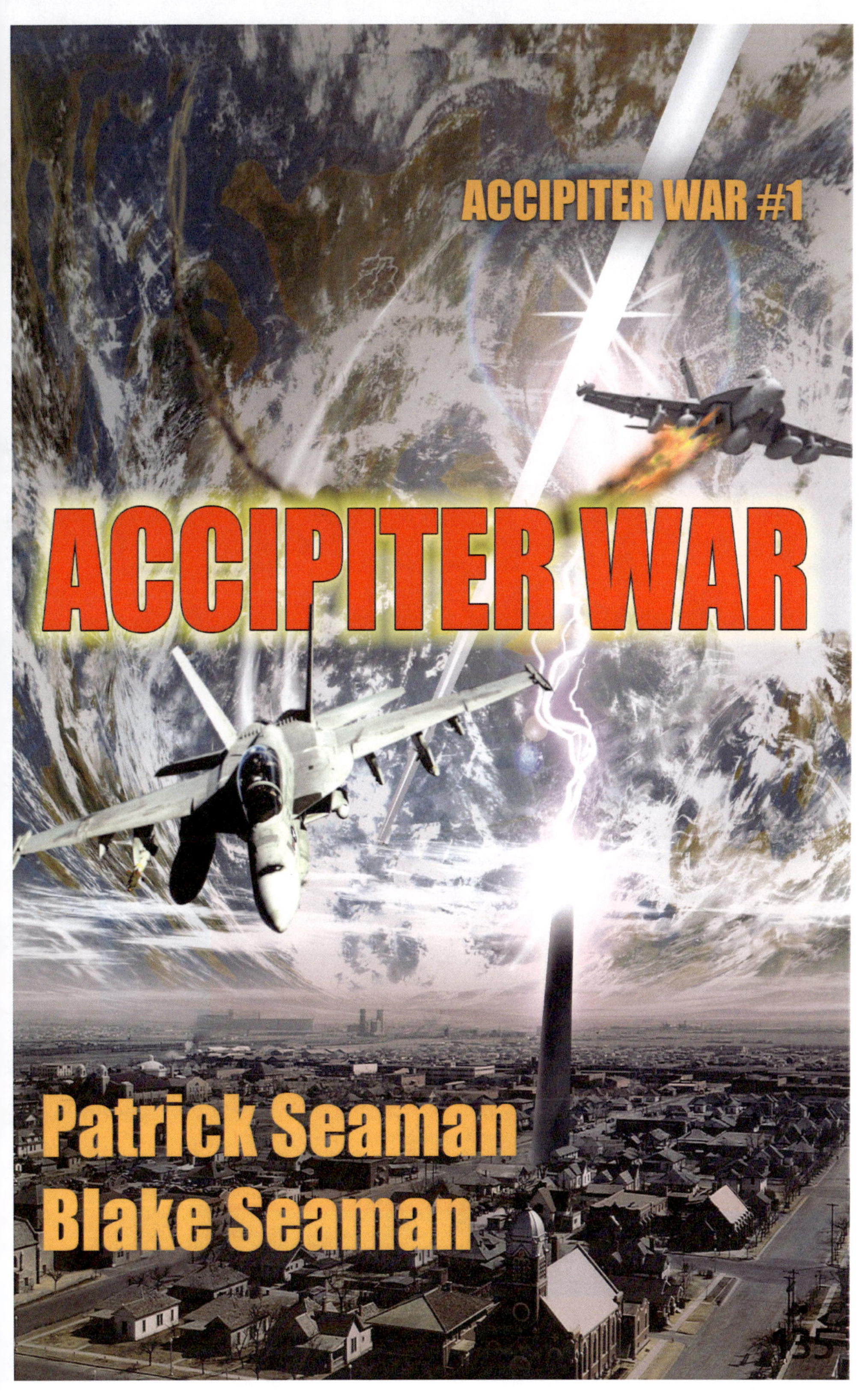
ACCIPITER WAR #1
ACCIPITER WAR
Patrick Seaman
Blake Seaman

Accipiter War #2
STEALING FIRE
Patrick Seaman
Blake Seaman

ACCIPITER WAR #4
HERETIC
PATRICK SEAMAN
BLAKE SEAMAN

Distribution: Ingram, Amazon,
Barnes & Noble, etc. Signed books
available at MilStar Books.com

MilstarBooks.com
Follow Patrick Seaman at:
http://www.linkedin.com/in/patrickseaman
http://PatrickSeaman.com
https://MilstarBooks.com
https://twitter.com/PatrickSeaman
https://www.facebook.com/PatrickSeamanAuthor

patrick@AccipiterWar.com

Amazon Series Page
https://www.amazon.com/dp/
B08GCTNGZW

Amazon Author Page:
https://www.amazon.com/stores/Patrick-Seaman/author/B01EISMC1Y